THE STEADFAST TIN SOLDIER

HANS CHRISTIAN ANDERSEN
ILLUSTRATED BY GEORGES LEMOINE

CREATIVE EDITIONS

MANKATO

Once upon a time

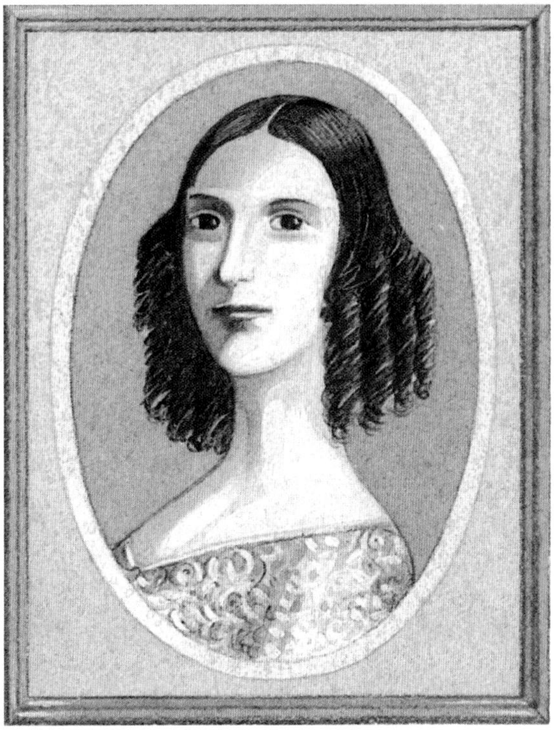

In 1840 Hans Christian
Andersen fell in love
with Jenny Lind,
the opera singer.
But they weren't able
to marry. Trying to
forget her, Andersen
began writing the
story of the tin soldier.
Was it him, the tin
soldier, hopelessly
in love with her,
the little dancer?

THERE were five-and-twenty tin soldiers—all brothers, as they were made out of the same old tin spoon. Their uniforms were red and blue, and they shouldered their guns and looked straight in front of them. The first words that they heard in this world, when the lid of the box in which they lay was taken off, were: "Hurrah, tin soldiers!" This was exclaimed by a little boy, clapping his hands; they had been given to him because it was his birthday, and now he began setting them out on the table. Each soldier was exactly like the other in shape, except just one, who had been made last when the tin had run short; but there he stood as firmly on his one leg as the others did on two, and he is the one that became famous.

There were many other playthings on the table on which they were being set out, but the nicest of all was a pretty little castle made of cardboard, with windows through which you could see into the rooms. In front of the castle stood some little trees surrounding a tiny mirror which looked like a lake. Wax swans were floating about and reflecting themselves in it. That was all very pretty, but the most beautiful thing was a little lady, who stood in the open doorway. She was cut out of paper, but she had on a dress of the finest cotton, with a scarf of narrow blue ribbon round her shoulders, fastened in the middle with a glittering rose made of gold paper, which was as large as her head. The little lady was stretching out both her arms, for she was a dancer, and was lifting up one leg so high in the air that the Tin Soldier couldn't see it and thought that she, too, had only one leg.

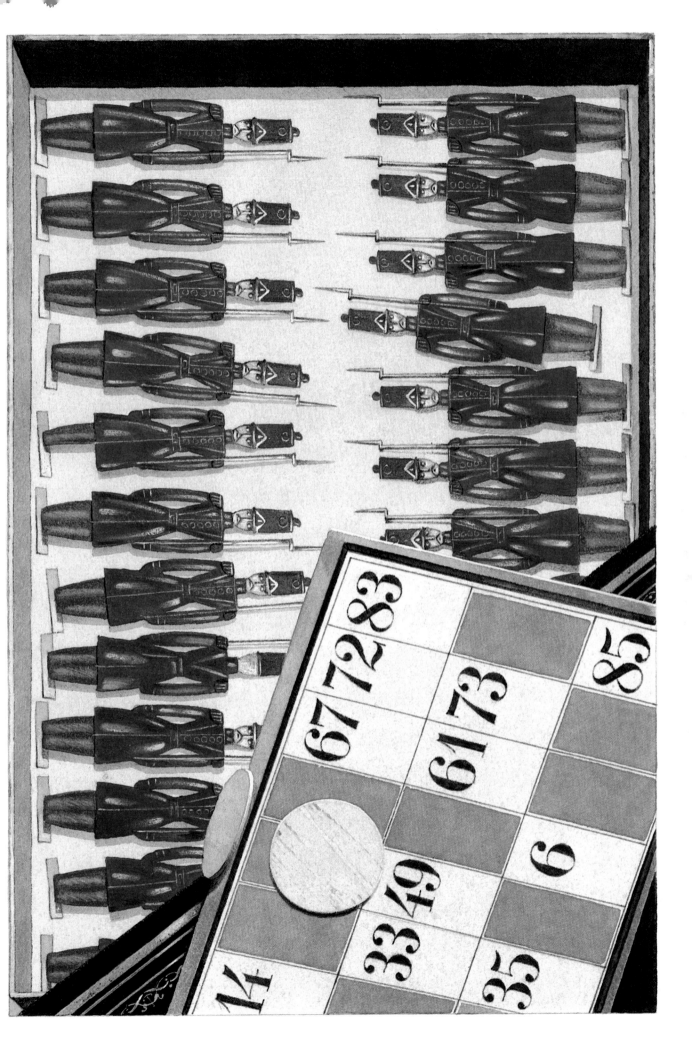

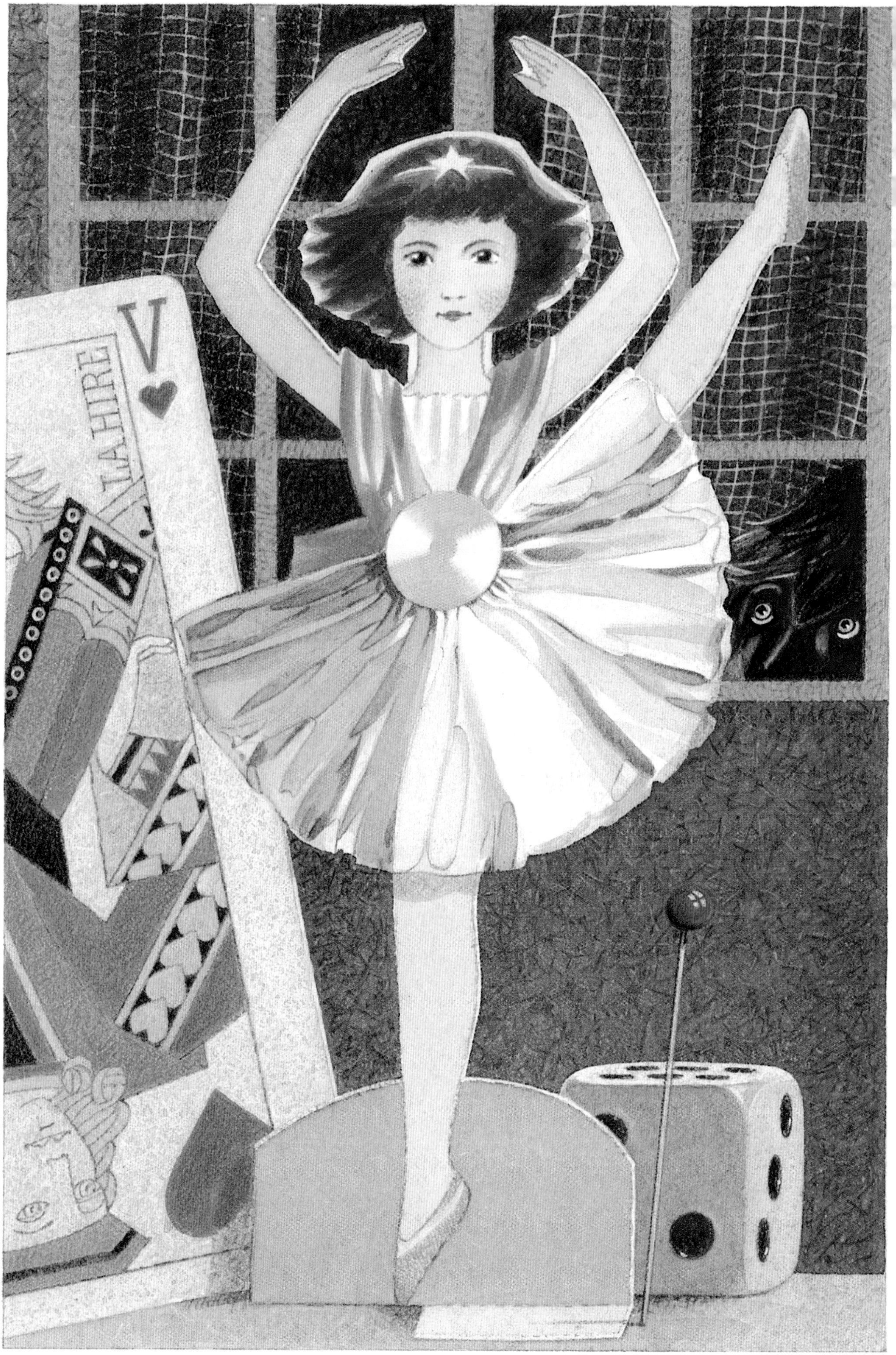
V
LAHIRE

"That's the wife for me!" he thought. "But she is so grand, and lives in a castle, while I have only a box with four-and-twenty others. This is no place for her! But I must make her acquaintance." Then he stretched himself out behind a snuffbox and watched the dainty lady, who continued to stand on one leg without losing her balance.

When the night came, all the other tin soldiers went into their box, and the people of the house went to bed. Then the toys began to play at visiting, dancing, and fighting. The tin soldiers rattled in their box, for they wanted to be out too, but they could not raise the lid. The nutcrackers played leapfrog, and the chalk ran about the chalkboard; there was such a noise that the canary woke up and began to talk in poetry! The only two who did not stir from their places were the Tin Soldier and the little Dancer. She remained on tiptoe, with both arms outstretched; he stood steadfastly on his one leg, never taking his eyes from her face.

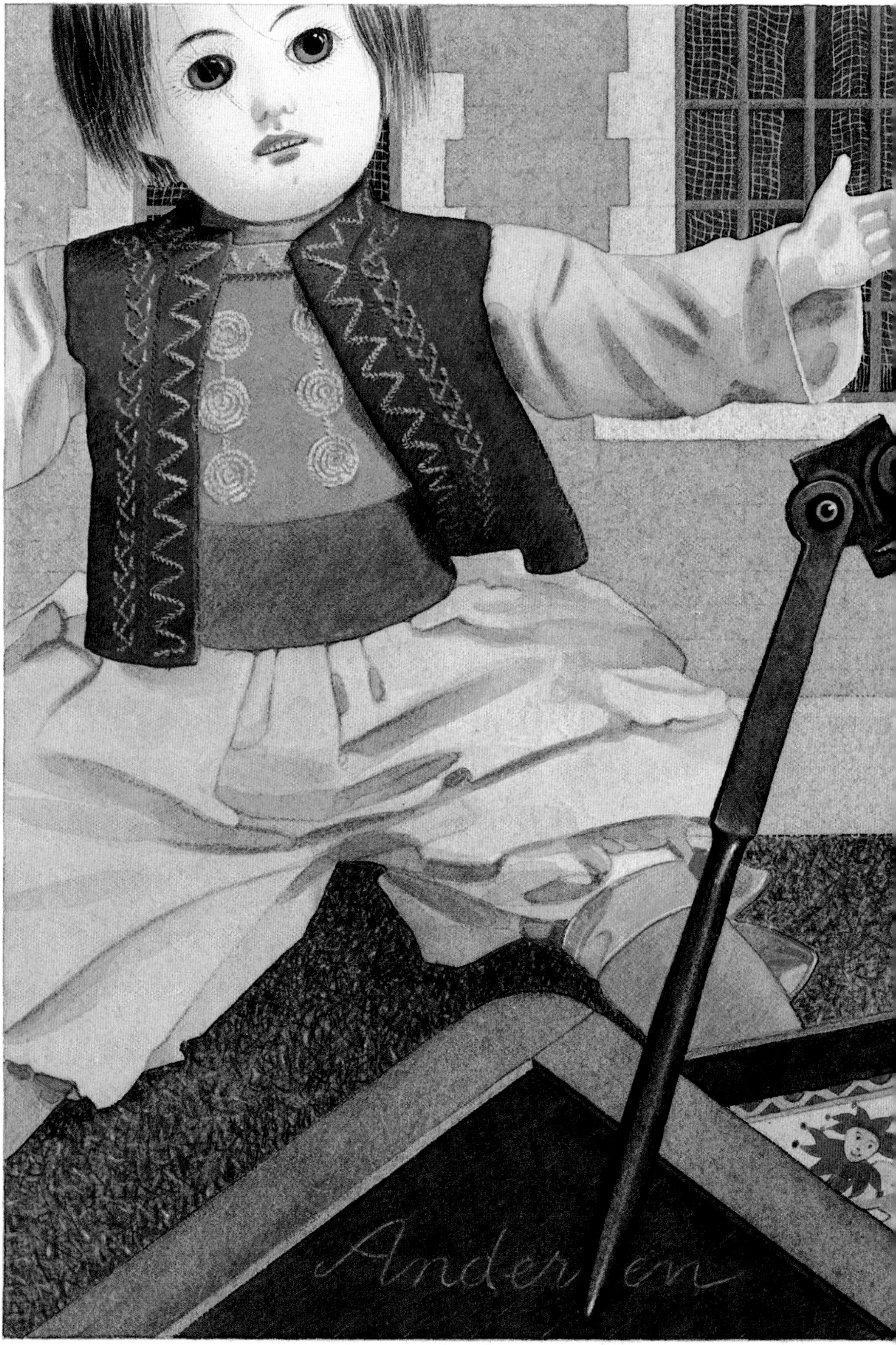
Ander en

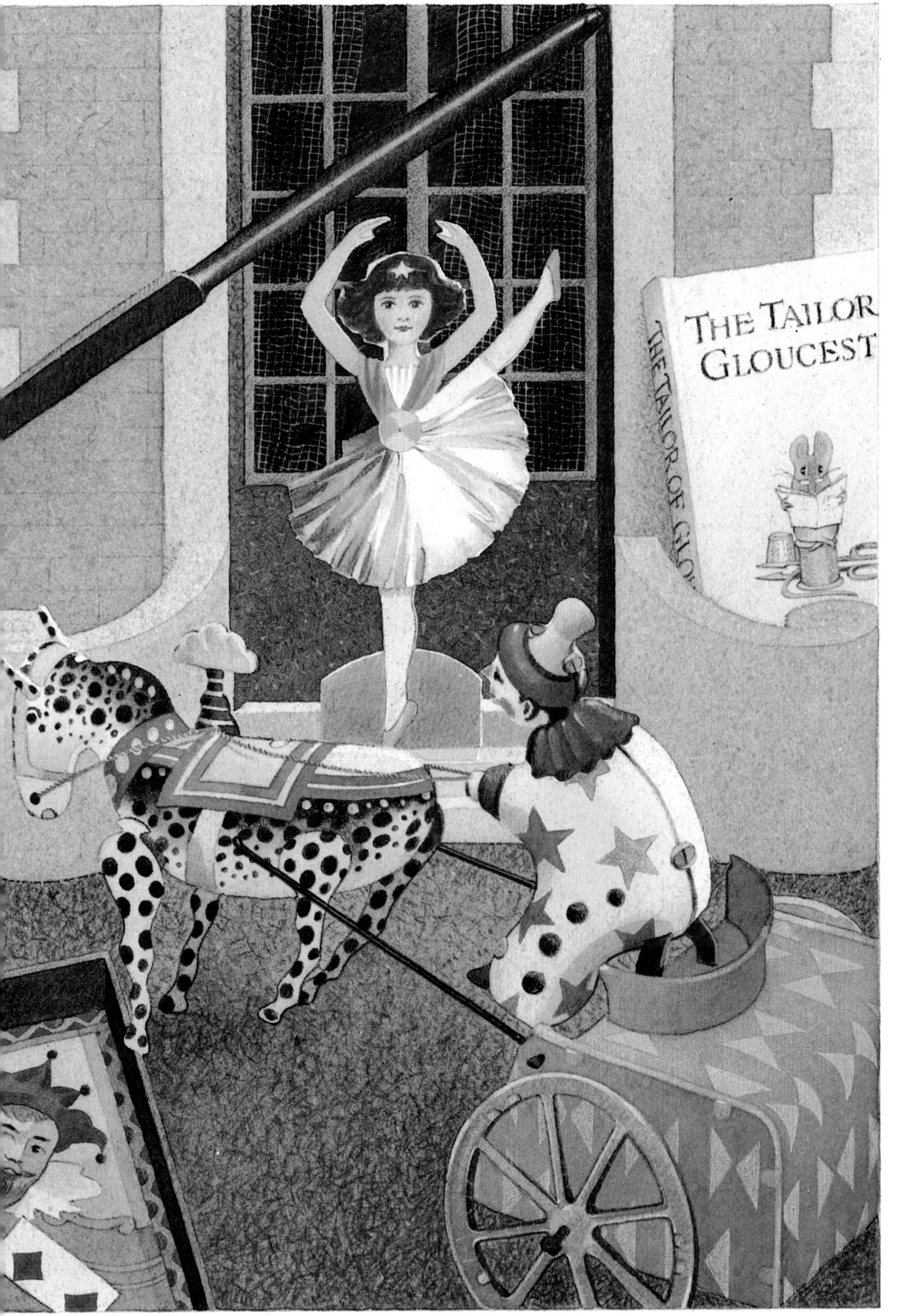
THE TAILOR
GLOUCEST
THE TAILOR OF GLO

The clock struck twelve, and crack! off flew the lid of the snuffbox. But there was no snuff inside, only a little black imp.

"Hello, Tin Soldier!" said the imp. "Don't look at things that aren't intended for the likes of you!"

But the Tin Soldier took no notice and seemed not to hear.

"Very well, wait till tomorrow!" said the imp.

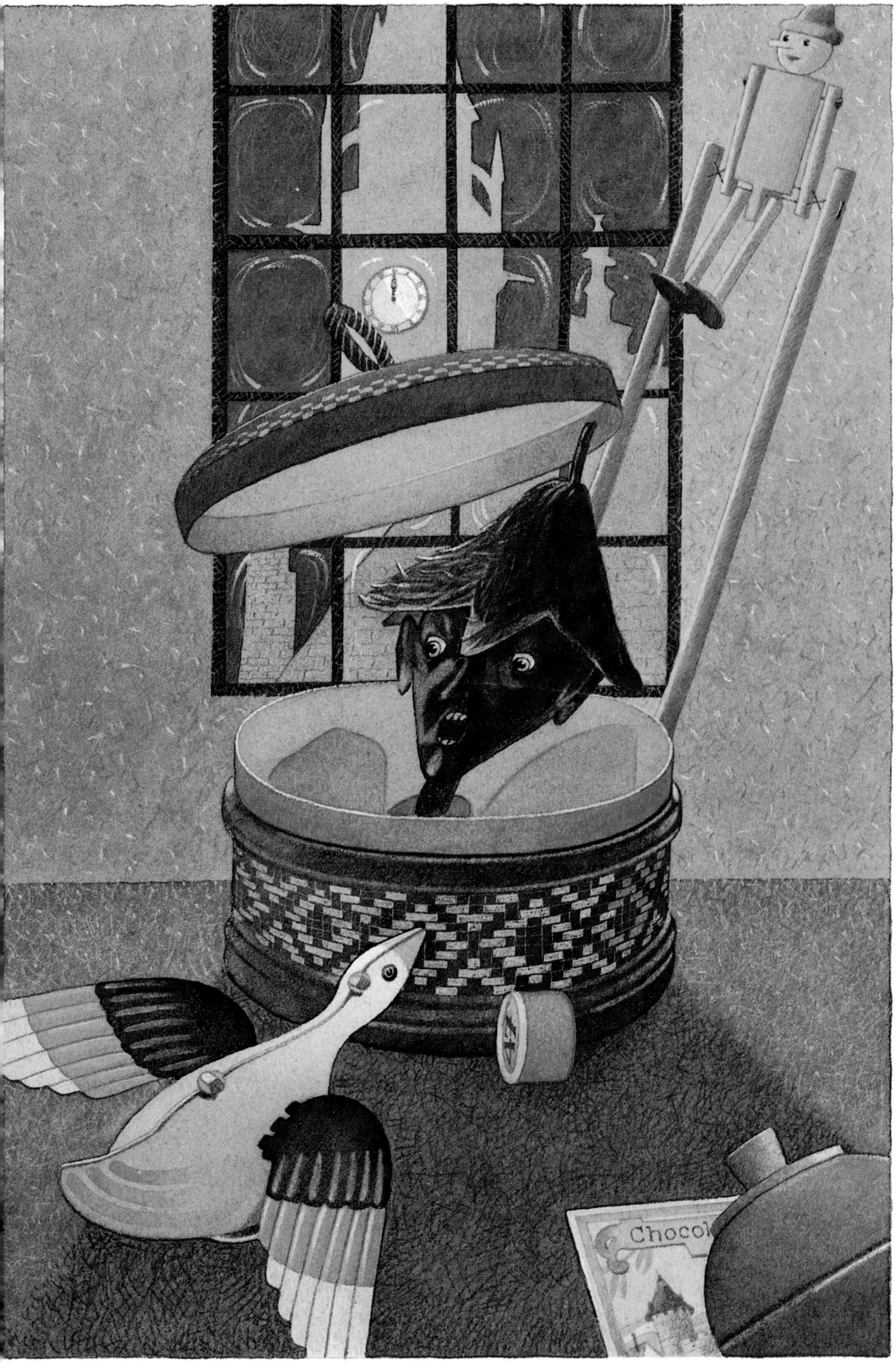
Chocol

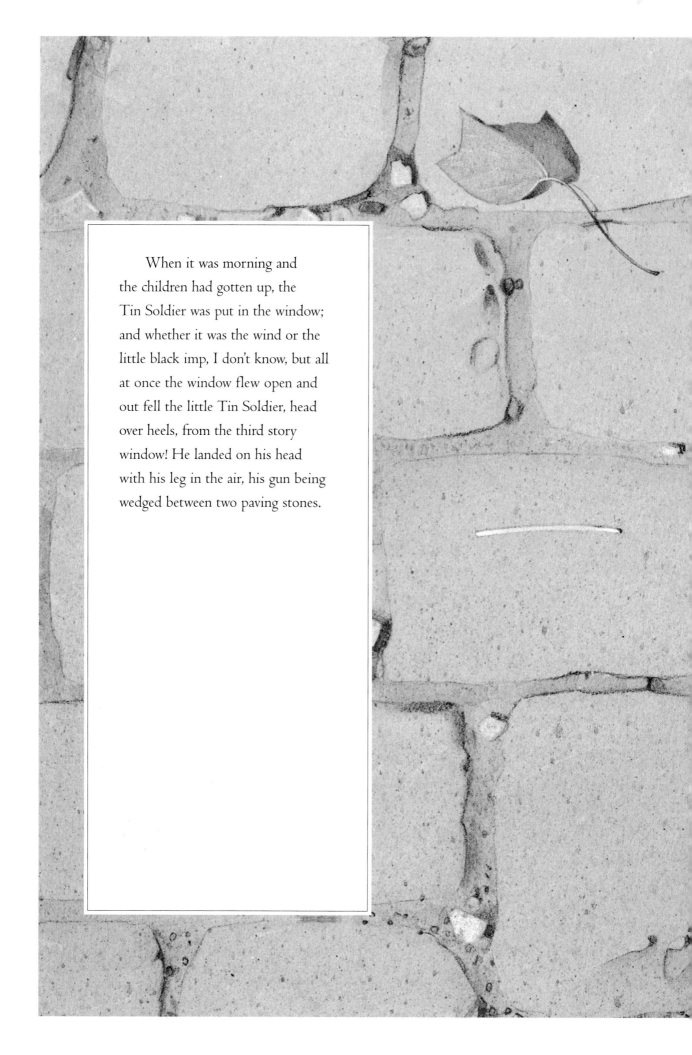

When it was morning and
the children had gotten up, the
Tin Soldier was put in the window;
and whether it was the wind or the
little black imp, I don't know, but all
at once the window flew open and
out fell the little Tin Soldier, head
over heels, from the third story
window! He landed on his head
with his leg in the air, his gun being
wedged between two paving stones.

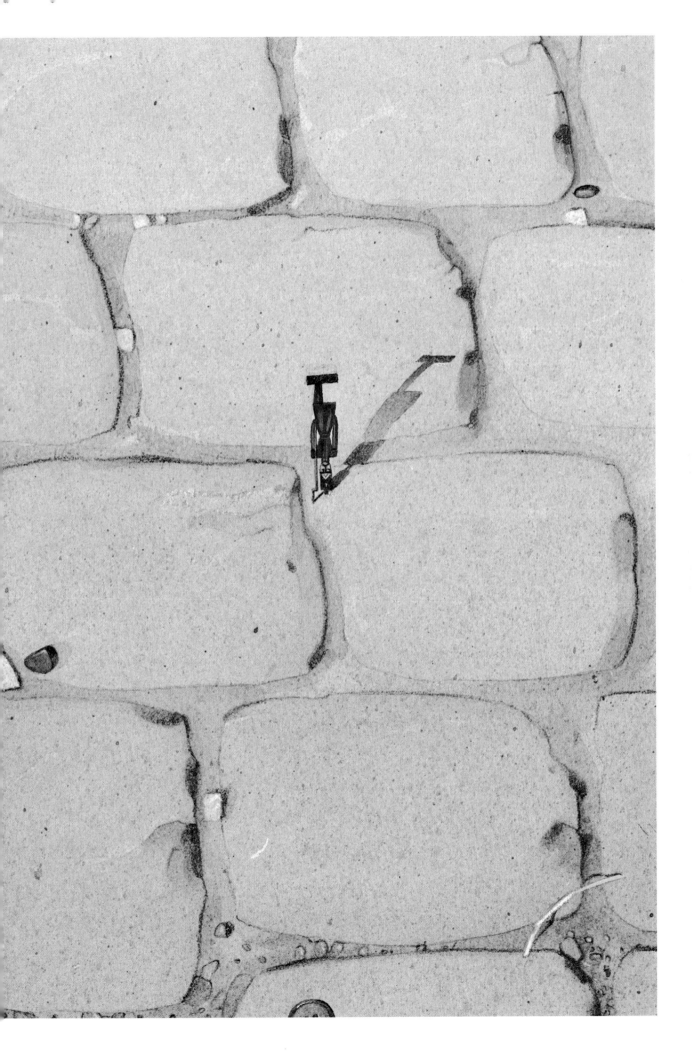

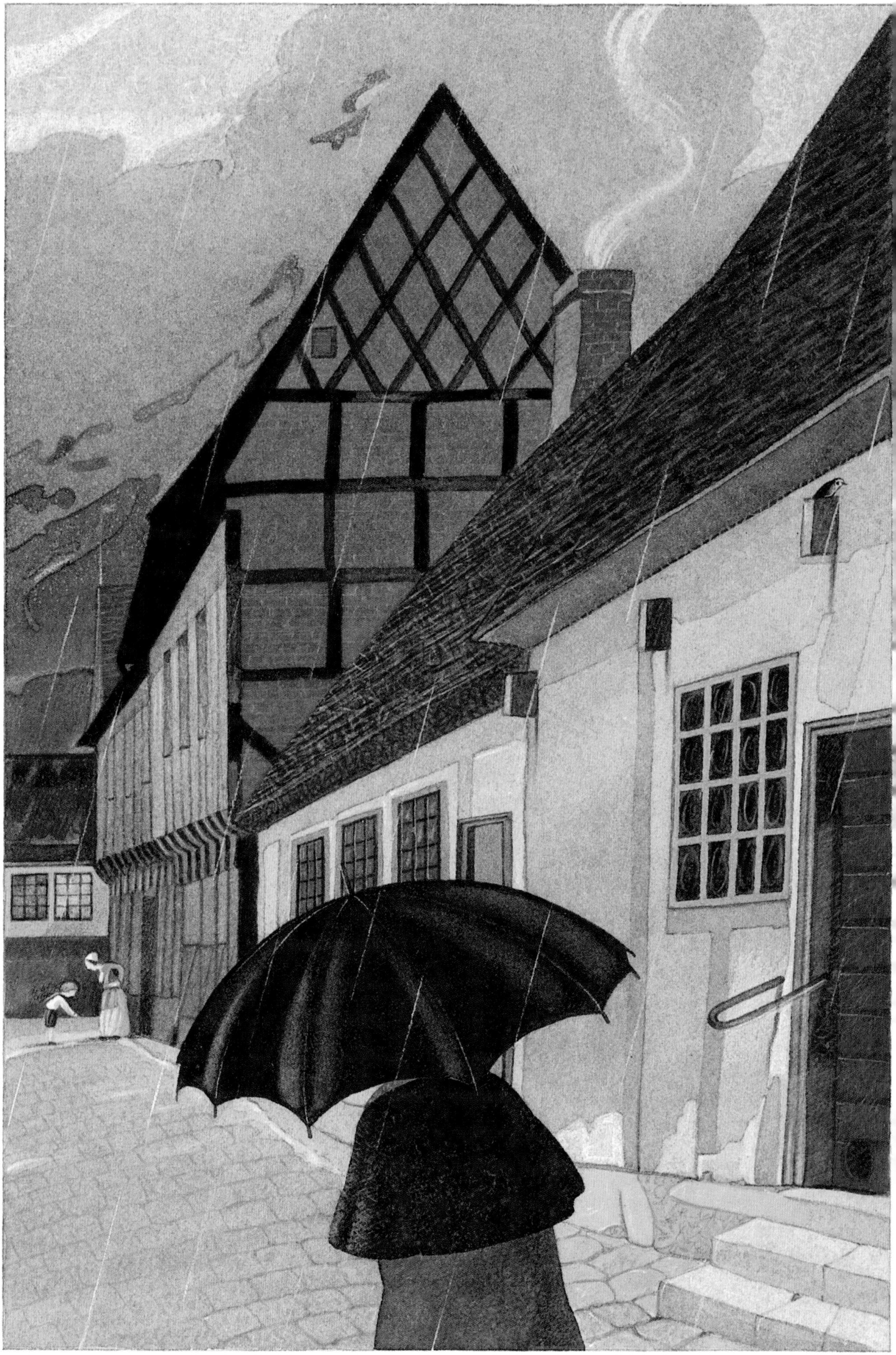

The nurserymaid and the little boy came down at once to look for him, but, though they were so near that they almost stepped on him, they did not notice him. If the Tin Soldier had only called out "Here I am!" they would have found him; but he did not think it fitting for him to cry out, because he had on his uniform.

Soon it began to drizzle; then the drops came faster, and there was a regular downpour. When it was over, two little street boys came along.

"Just look!" cried one. "Here is a tin soldier! He shall sail up and down in a boat!"

So they made a little boat out of newspaper, put the Tin Soldier in it, and made him sail up and down the gutter; the boys ran along beside him, clapping their hands. What great waves there were in the gutter, and what a swift current! The paper boat tossed up and down, and in the middle of the stream it went so quick that the Tin Soldier trembled; but he remained steadfast and looked straight in front of him, shouldering his gun.

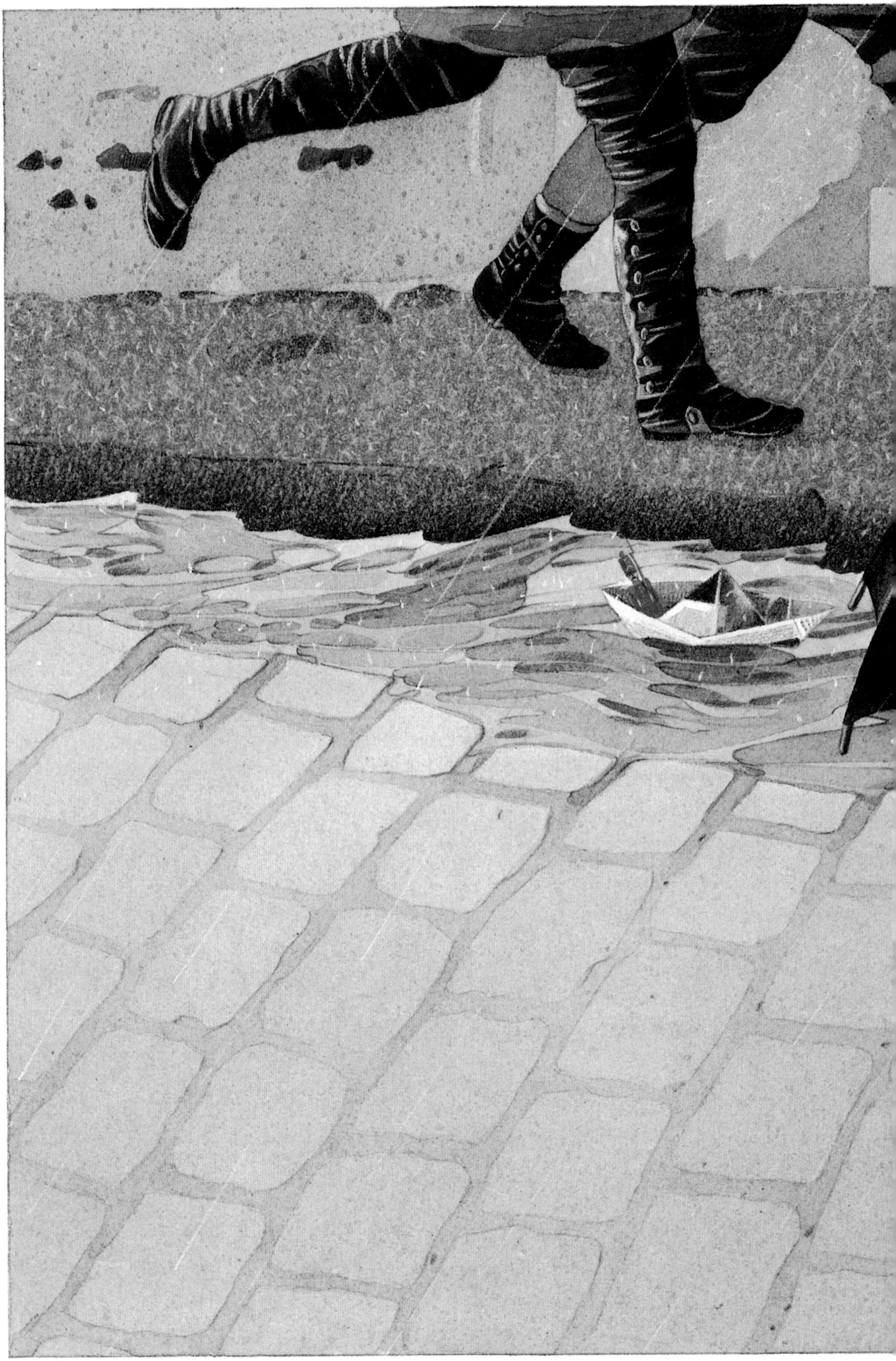

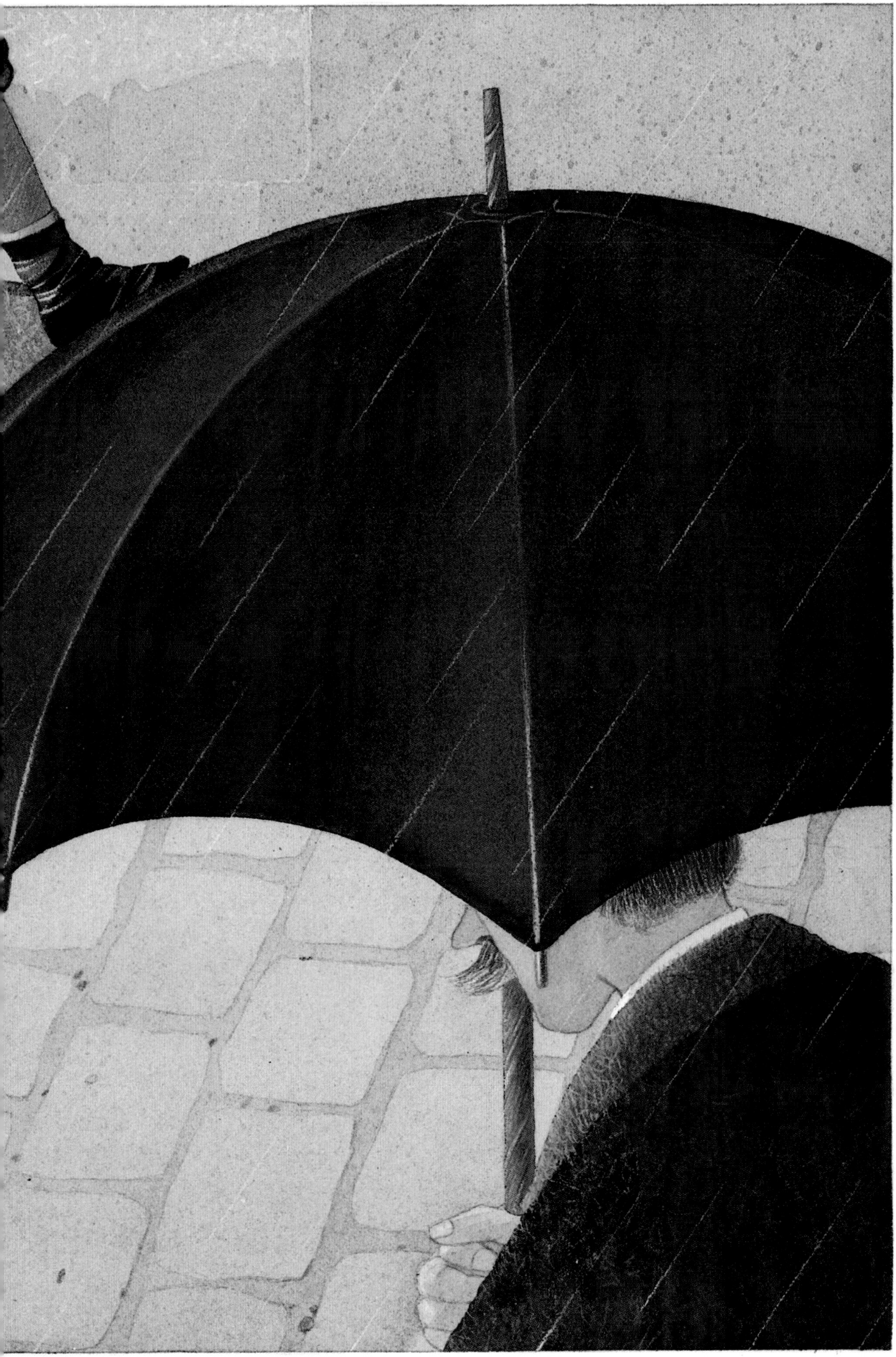

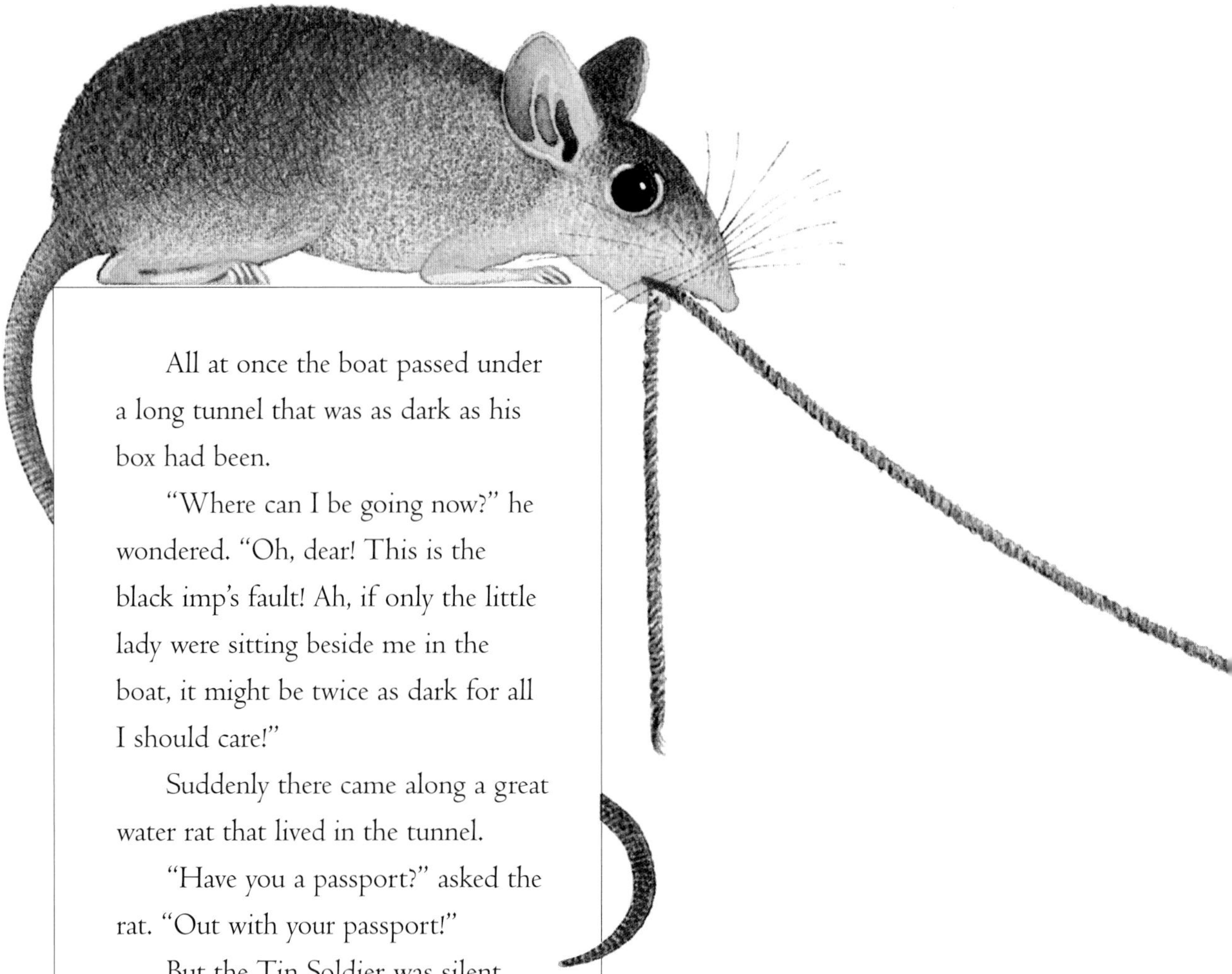

All at once the boat passed under a long tunnel that was as dark as his box had been.

"Where can I be going now?" he wondered. "Oh, dear! This is the black imp's fault! Ah, if only the little lady were sitting beside me in the boat, it might be twice as dark for all I should care!"

Suddenly there came along a great water rat that lived in the tunnel.

"Have you a passport?" asked the rat. "Out with your passport!"

But the Tin Soldier was silent and grasped his gun more firmly.

The boat sped on, with the rat behind it. Ugh! How he showed his teeth as he cried to the chips of wood and straw: "Hold him, hold him! He has not paid the toll! He has not shown his passport!"

But the current became swifter. The Tin Soldier could already see daylight where the tunnel ended; but in his ears there sounded a roaring enough to frighten any brave man.

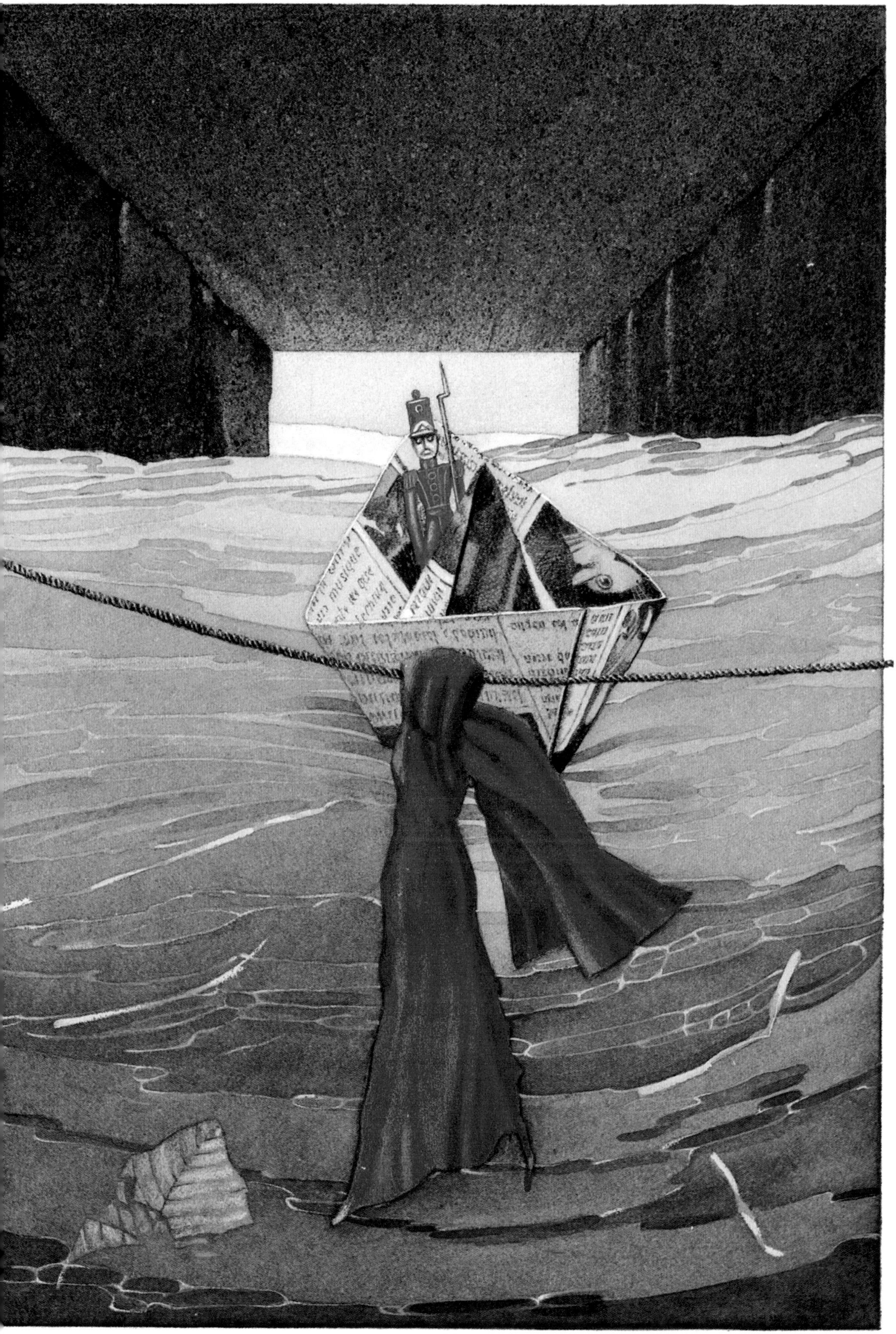
musique

Then the Tin Soldier saw that at the end of the tunnel the gutter discharged itself into a great canal; that would be just as dangerous for him as a waterfall would be for a human.

Now he was so near to it that he could not hold on any longer. On went the boat, the poor Tin Soldier keeping himself as stiff as he could so that no one should say of him afterwards that he had flinched. The boat whirled three, four times round, and became filled to the brim with water; at last it began to sink! The Tin Soldier was standing up to his neck in water, and deeper and deeper sank the boat, and softer and softer grew the paper; then the water was over his head.

He was thinking of the pretty little Dancer, whose face he should never see again, and there sounded in his ears, over and over again:

> "Forward, forward,
> Soldier bold!
> Death's before thee,
> Grim and cold!"

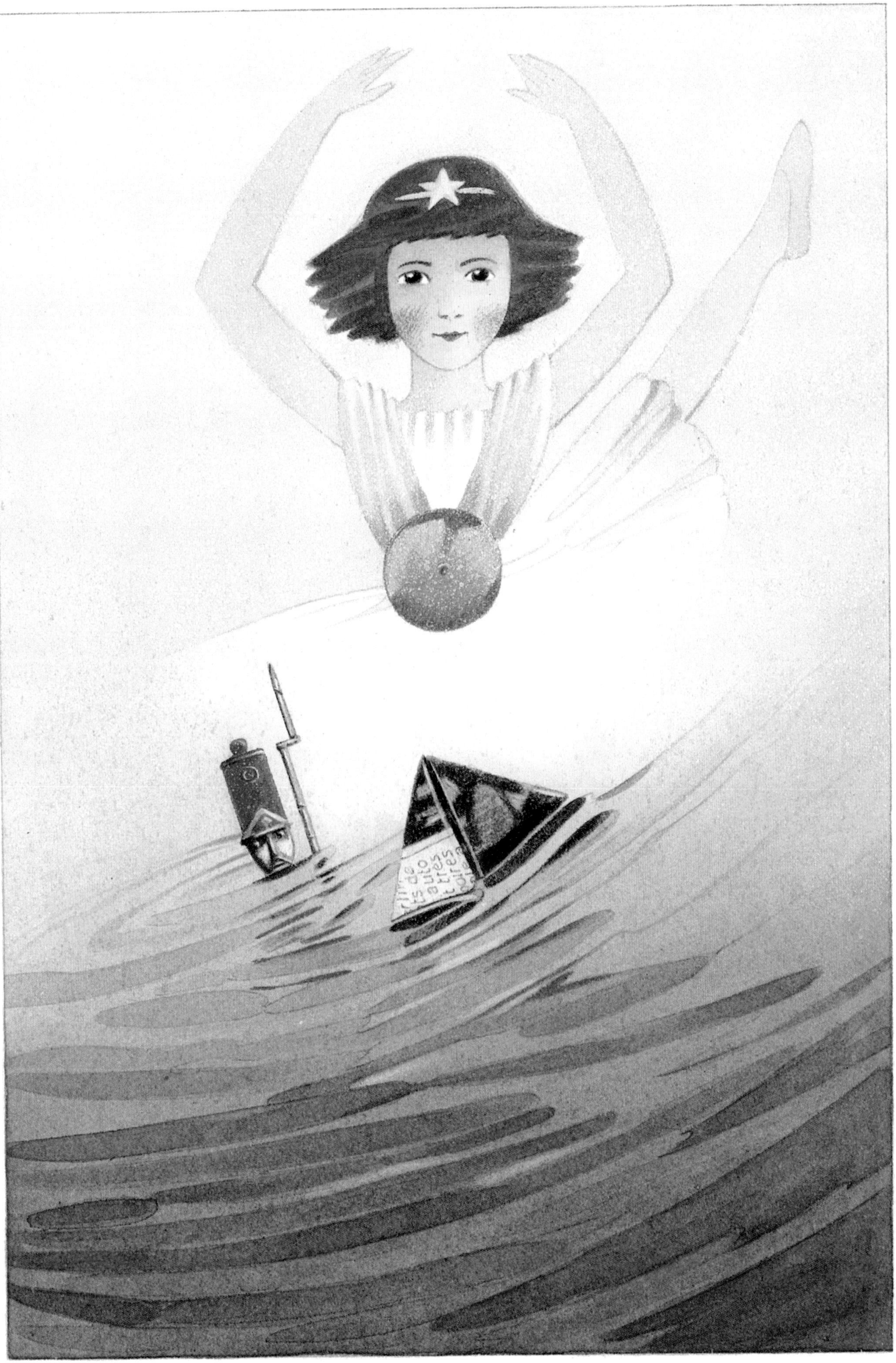

The paper finally tore in two, and the soldier fell—but at that moment he was swallowed by a great fish.

Oh! How dark it was inside, even darker than in the tunnel, and it was really very close quarters! But there the steadfast little Tin Soldier lay full length, shouldering his gun.

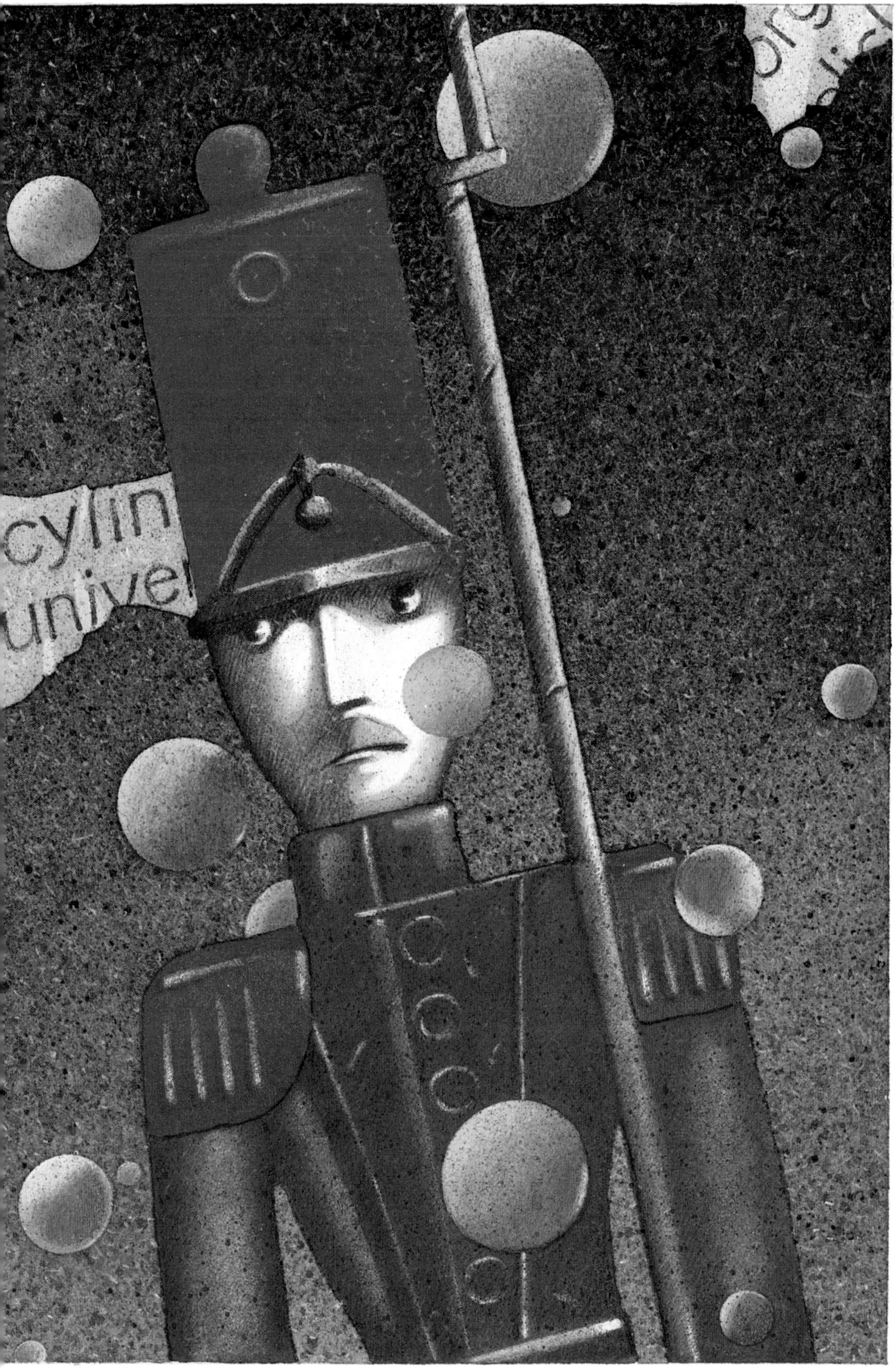
cylin
unive

Up and down swam the fish, then he made the most dreadful contortions and became suddenly quite still. Then it was as if a flash of lightning had passed through him; daylight streamed in, and a voice exclaimed, "Why, here is a little tin soldier!" The fish had been caught, taken to market, sold, and brought into the kitchen, where the cook had cut it open with a great sharp knife.

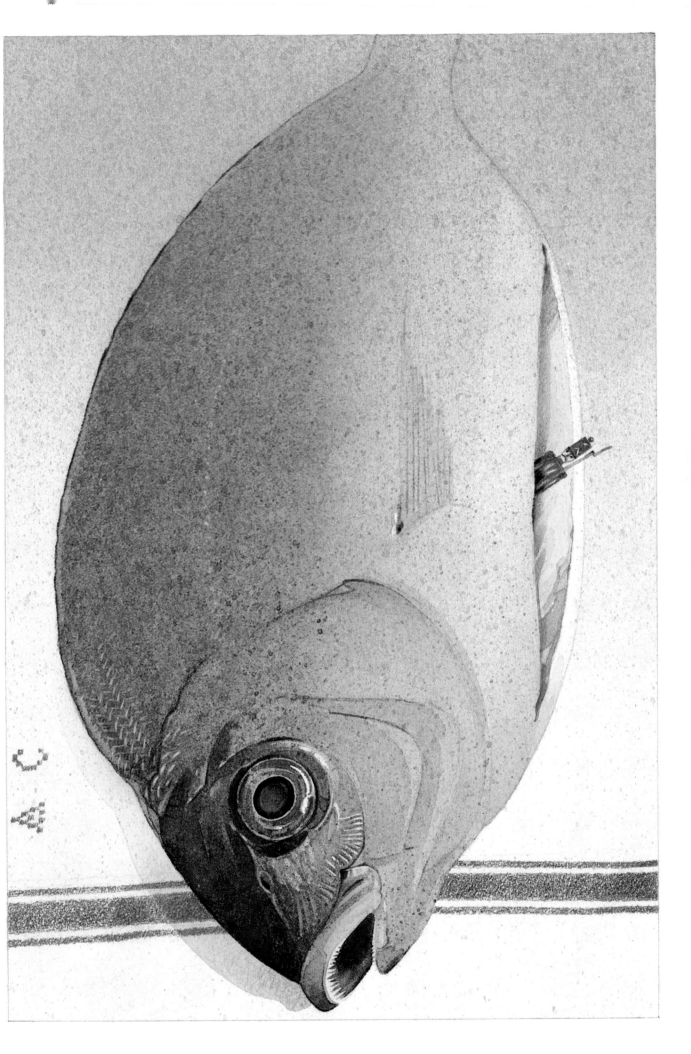

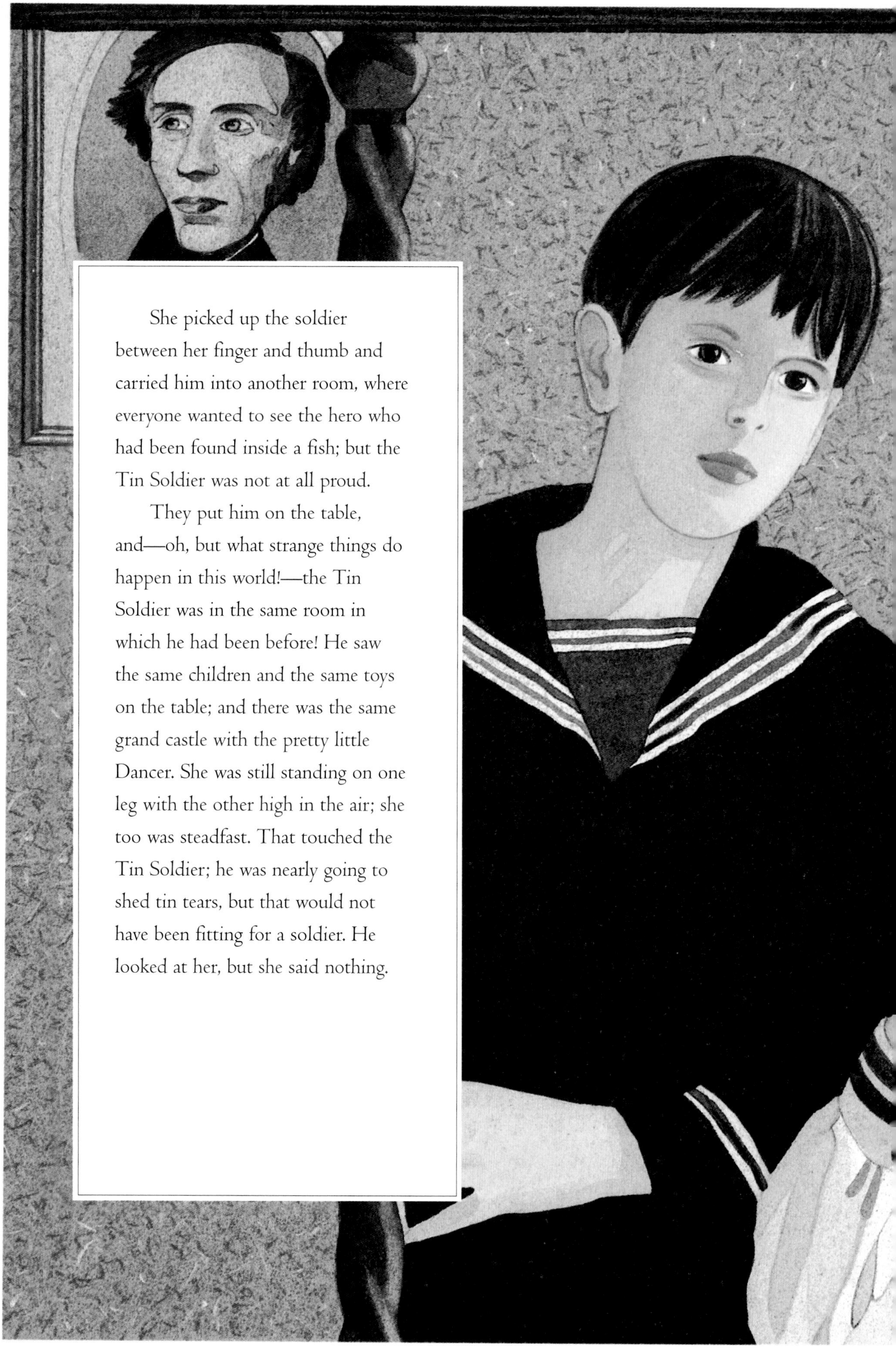

She picked up the soldier between her finger and thumb and carried him into another room, where everyone wanted to see the hero who had been found inside a fish; but the Tin Soldier was not at all proud.

They put him on the table, and—oh, but what strange things do happen in this world!—the Tin Soldier was in the same room in which he had been before! He saw the same children and the same toys on the table; and there was the same grand castle with the pretty little Dancer. She was still standing on one leg with the other high in the air; she too was steadfast. That touched the Tin Soldier; he was nearly going to shed tin tears, but that would not have been fitting for a soldier. He looked at her, but she said nothing.

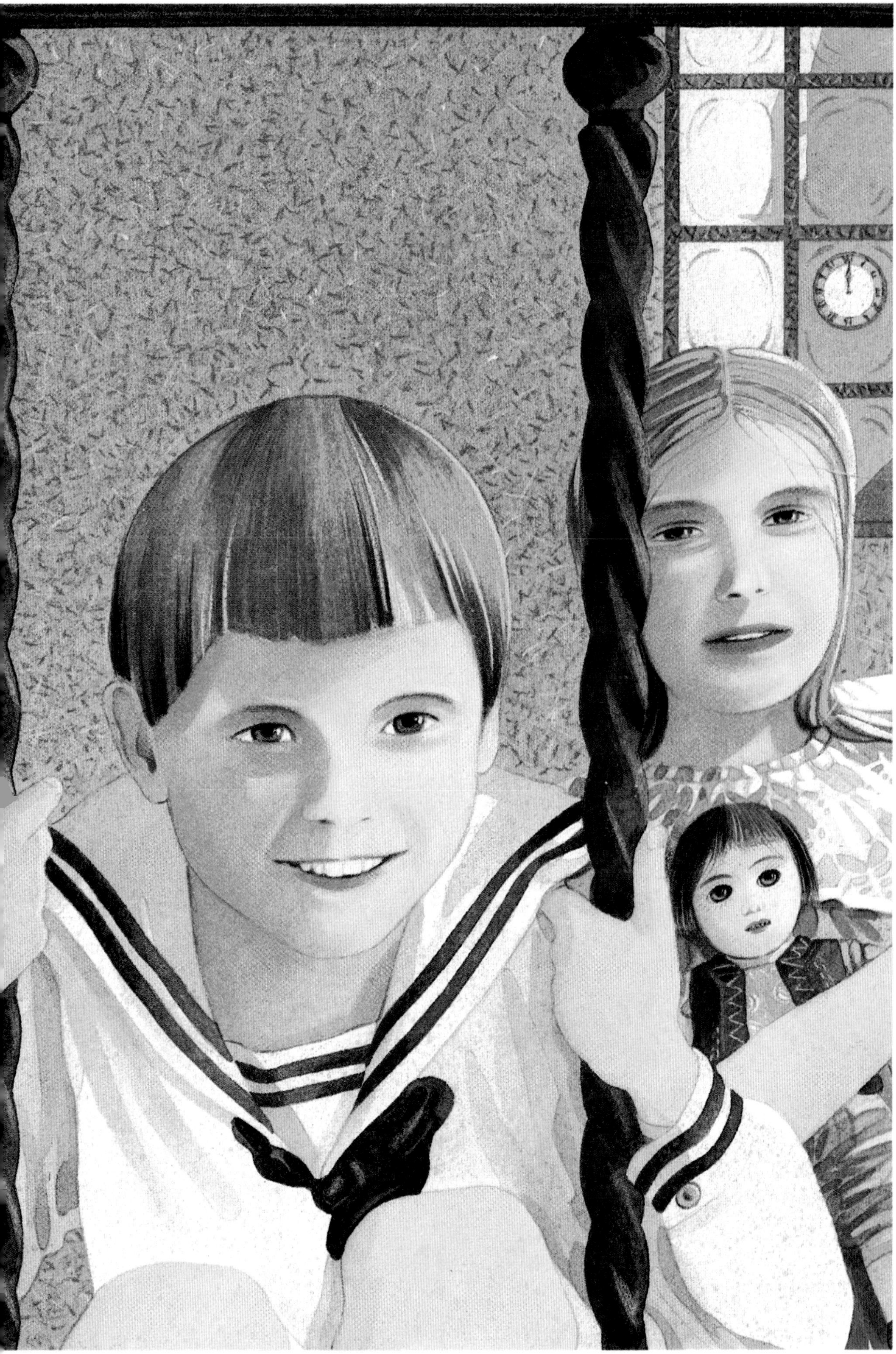

All at once, one of the little boys
picked up the Tin Soldier and threw
him into the stove, giving no reasons;
but doubtless the little black imp in the
snuffbox was at the bottom of this too.

There the Tin Soldier lay and felt a
heat that was truly terrible; but whether
he was suffering from actual fire or from
the ardor of his passion he did not know.
All his color had disappeared; whether
this had happened on his travels or
because of the great heat, who can say?

He looked at the little lady, she
looked at him, and he felt that he was
melting; but he remained steadfast, with
his gun at his shoulder. Suddenly a door
opened, the draft caught up the little
Dancer, and off she flew to the Tin
Soldier in the stove, burst into flames—
and that was the end of her! Then the
Tin Soldier melted down into a little
lump, and when the maid was taking out
the ashes the next morning, she found
him in the shape of a heart. There was
nothing left of the little Dancer but her
gold rose, burnt as black as a cinder.

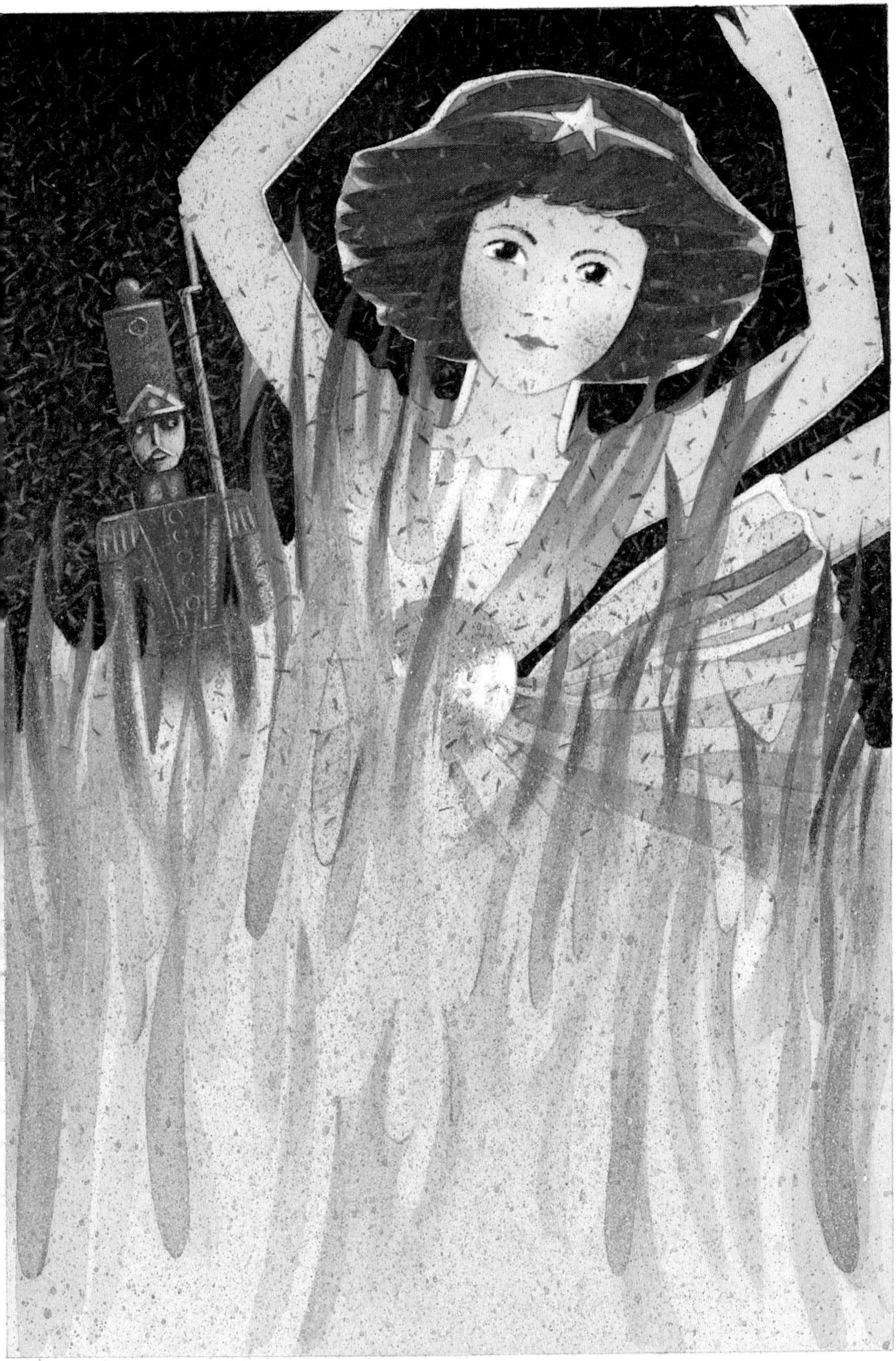